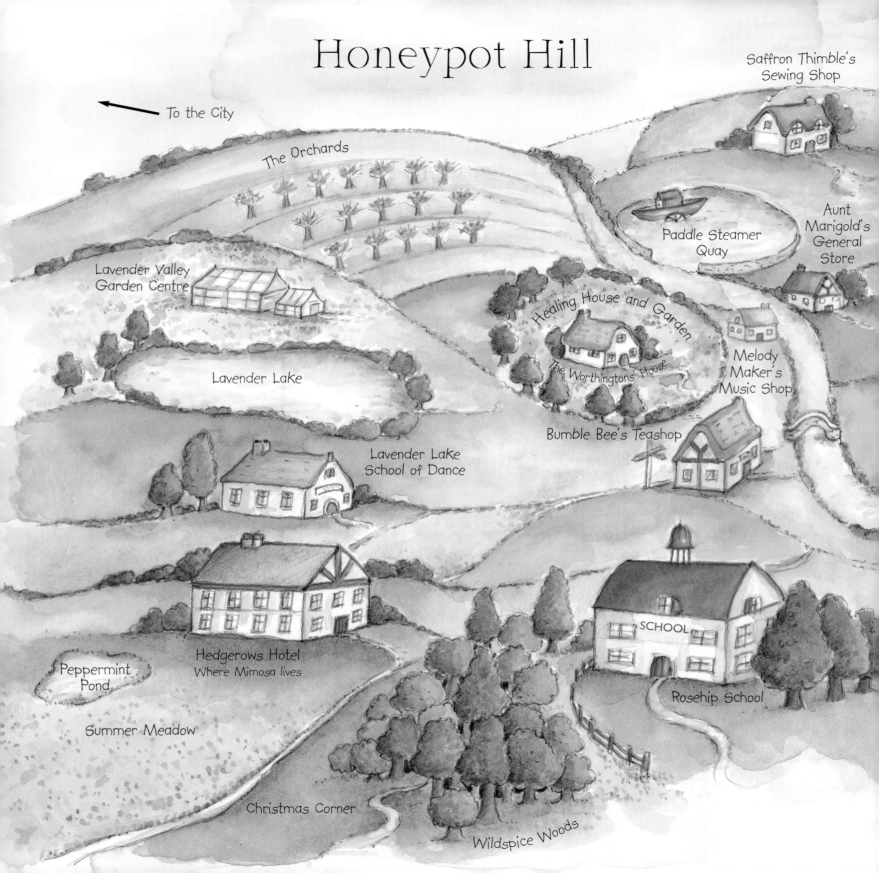

Honeypot Hill

Saffron Thimble's Sewing Shop

To the City

The Orchards

Paddle Steamer Quay

Aunt Marigold's General Store

Lavender Valley Garden Centre

Healing House and Garden

The Worthingtons' House

Melody Maker's Music Shop

Lavender Lake

Lavender Lake School of Dance

Bumble Bee's Teashop

Peppermint Pond

Hedgerows Hotel
Where Mimosa lives

SCHOOL

Rosehip School

Summer Meadow

Christmas Corner

Wildspice Woods

Honeysuckle Cottage
Poppy's House

Forget-Me-Not Cottage
Grandpa's House and Office

Poppy Field

Honeypot Cottage
Honey and Granny Bumble's House

Blossom
Bakehouse

Cornsilk Castle
and Courtyard

Village Hall

Sage's
Vet Surgery

Post Office

Beehive
Beauty Salon

River Swan

Barley Farm
The Meadowsweets' House

Riverside
Stables

Honeypot Hill
Railway Station

To Camomile Cove
via Periwinkle Lane

N
W   E
S

*Visit Princess Poppy for fun, games, puzzles,
activities, downloads and lots more at*

www.princesspoppy.com

FLOWER PRINCESS
A PICTURE CORGI BOOK 978 0 552 56192 1

First published in Great Britain by Picture Corgi,
an imprint of Random House Children's Books
A Random House Group Company

This edition published 2010

1 3 5 7 9 10 8 6 4 2

Text copyright © Janey Louise Jones, 2010
Illustrations copyright © Picture Corgi Books, 2010
Illustrations by Veronica Vasylenko
Design by Tracey Cunnell

Picture Corgi Books are published by Random House Children's Books,
61–63 Uxbridge Road, London W5 5SA

Addresses for companies within The Random House Group Limited
can be found at: www.randomhouse.co.uk/offices.htm

www.princesspoppy.com
www.kidsatrandomhouse.co.uk
www.rbooks.co.uk

THE RANDOM HOUSE GROUP Limited Reg. No. 954009

A CIP catalogue record for this book is available from the British Library

Printed in China

Flower Princess

Written by Janey Louise Jones

PICTURE CORGI

With love to Sophia Dickson,
a little princess

★

Flower Princess

featuring

Grandpa
★

Princess Poppy

Mum
★

Saffron
★

Honey
★

Granny Bumble
★

"Were there any princesses in Honeypot Hill when you were my age, Grandpa?" asked Poppy as they strolled through Summer Meadow.

"There certainly were! Every year, when the wild flowers came out, all the girls would dress up as princesses and dance through this meadow! It was a lovely village tradition — I wish we still did it."

"Wow! That sounds really fun!" said Poppy.

When she got home she found Mum and the twins in the garden.

"Hi, Poppy," called Mum. "It's Grandpa's birthday on Saturday and I want to organize something special."

Poppy was bursting with excitement.

"I hope Grandpa likes it!" she said to Honey as the girls linked hands and ran to hide behind an oak tree.

"SURPRISE!" called all the flower princesses
as they skipped out to meet Grandpa.

"Happy Birthday!"

"Thank you!" beamed Grandpa. "I am a silly old fool – I thought you had all forgotten!"

"We would never forget your special day, Grandpa!" replied Poppy.

"Oh, and we've got another surprise for you," said Poppy. "Watch this!"

The girls performed their princess dance under flower archways.

Grandpa clapped his hands.

"Thank you! This has been the best birthday ever!"

When the party was over Poppy and Grandpa sat down together.

"You know, every girl in this village is a princess but you are the number one princess as far as I am concerned!"

"Thank you!" smiled Poppy. "Did you like your surprise?"

"I've loved my day, darling. You're never too old for birthdays, you know!"